P9-DTR-408

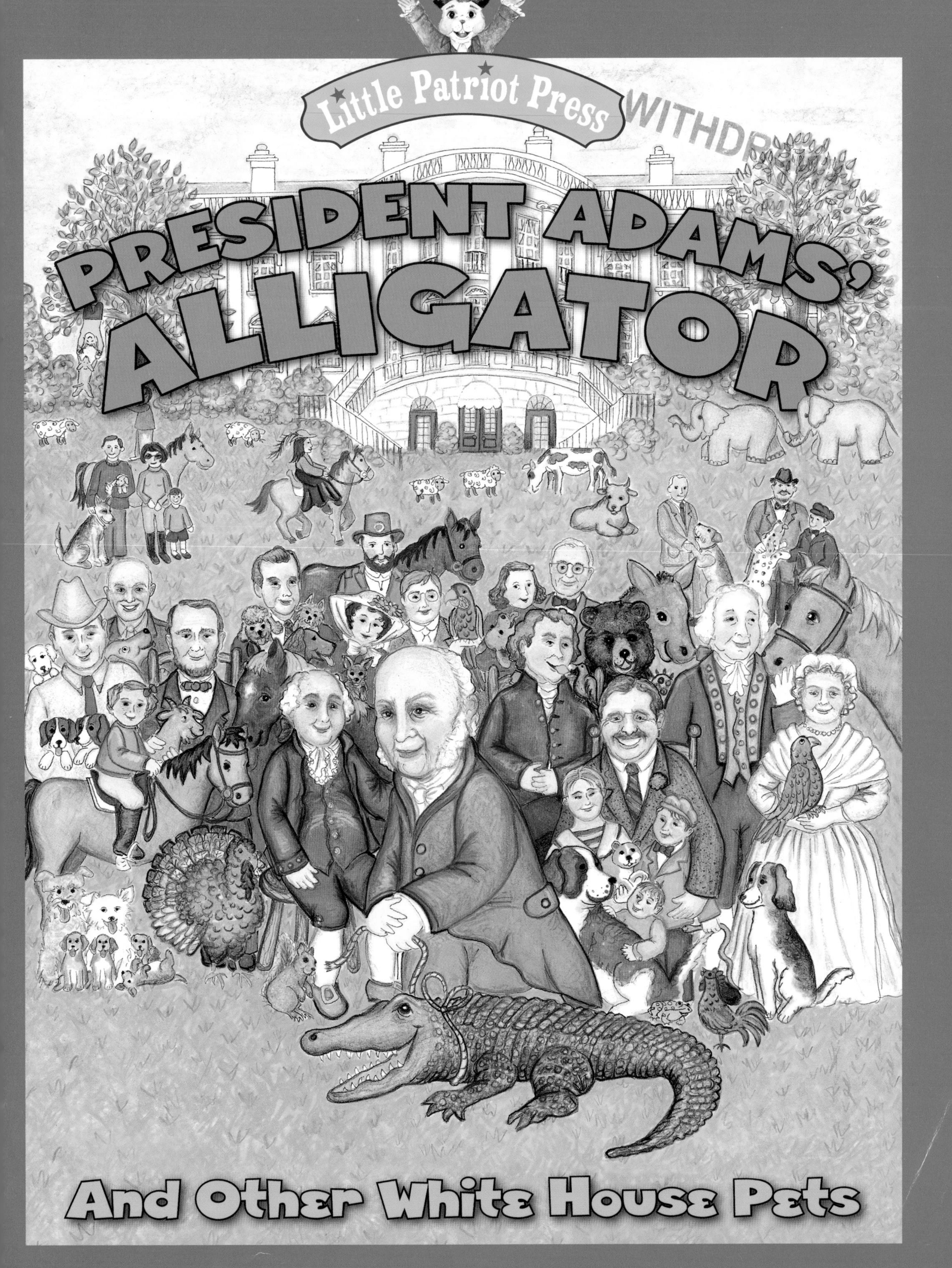

By Peter W. Barnes and Cheryl Shaw Barnes

Library of Congress Control Number: 2012946829
ISBN 978-1-62157-035-6

Published in the United States by
Little Patriot Press
an imprint of Regnery Publishing, Inc.
One Massachusetts Avenue, NW
Washington, DC 20001
www.Regnery.com

Manufactured in the United States of America
10 9 8 7 6 5 4 3 2 1

Books are available in quantity for promotional or premium use. For information on discounts and terms write to Director of Special Sales, Regnery Publishing, Inc., One Massachusetts Avenue, NW, Washington, DC, 20001, or call 202-216-0600.

Distributed to the trade by:
Perseus Distribution
250 West 57th Street
New York, NY 10107

We dedicate this book to

The memory
of our father, Charles Stephen Shaw,
who was always our biggest fan—
We miss you, Dad!—and also to
Barbara and the late Buddy Miller,
who we love very much!

—P.W.B and C.S.B.

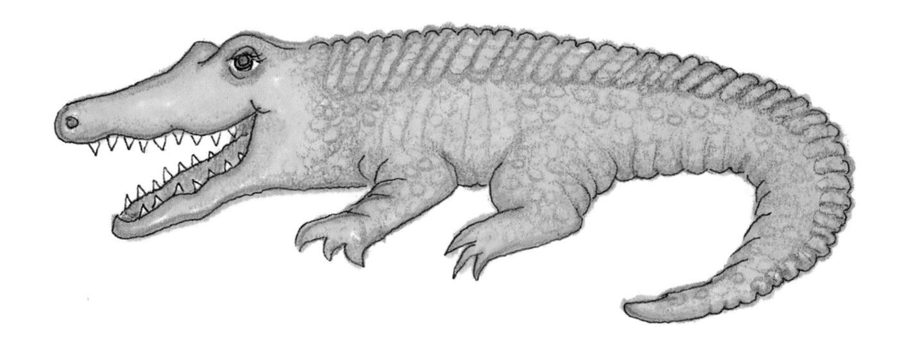

Look for **President Adams' alligator** hidden in every illustration in this book.

"What is your favorite pet?" Mrs. Tucker asked her class.

All the children answered at once: "A mouse!" "My kitty!" "A big snake!" "Ewww!" "My guinea pig!" "A pony!" "My dog, Juno!"

"Wow, those all sound like great pets," Mrs. Tucker said. She noticed Billy in the back of the room doodling on some paper. "Billy? I didn't hear from you. Don't you have a favorite pet?"

Billy looked up and smiled. “I am drawing my favorite pet.”

“Well, what is it?” Mrs. Tucker asked.

Billy picked up his picture and pointed to a bright green alligator with a big toothy grin.

“An alligator?!?” the kids screamed all at once. “An alligator isn’t a pet!”

“Now hold on a second, class,” Mrs. Tucker said. “An alligator can be a pet. Why, even one of our presidents had an alligator. In fact, the presidents had all kinds of pets—lots of dogs and cats, of course. But they also had some very strange pets.”

“Like what?” the children asked.

“Why don’t I tell you some stories about them? Then at the end of class, each of you can vote for your favorite presidential pet. How does that sound?”

“Great!” yelled the children.

“Our Founding Fathers loved animals. Did you know that our very first president, George Washington, had hunting dogs named Madame Moose, Sweetlips, and Tipsy? He also had many horses. His favorite was a big, strong horse named Nelson. President Washington wanted to make sure all his horses had nice, healthy teeth, so he had them brushed regularly. You would need a pretty big toothbrush for that job!

“Our second president, John Adams, loved horses too. He loved one horse so much that he had a stable built for her right on the White House lawn. Her name was Cleopatra.

“Our third president, Thomas Jefferson, had two pet grizzly bears! He also had a pet mockingbird named Dick. The president and Dick were very close. Jefferson would let Dick sit on his shoulder and eat food from his lips! Dick also liked to sing along when the president played his violin.

“Another bird in the White House was Polly. Polly the parrot was the pet of our fourth president, James Madison. President Madison also had a sheepdog.

“Clippety-clop, clippety-clop. Here come the presidents and their horses marching down the street to the sound of a beating drum. Everyone loves to show off his or her favorite pet. And what better way to show off a horse than in a parade? Andrew Jackson had horses named Sam Patches, Emily, and Lady Bolivia. He loved these horses, but his favorite pet was a parrot named Poll.

“President William Henry Harrison brought his cow, Sukey, with him to the White House.

“President John Tyler rode a horse named The General, and had two Italian wolfhounds.

“Zachary Taylor’s favorite horse, Old Whitey, liked to snack on the grass of the White House lawn. Poor Old Whitey didn’t have a very thick tail—visitors would sometimes pull out the hairs for souvenirs!

“Even an alligator once lived in the White House! Back in 1825, a man named General Lafayette brought an alligator to live with President John Quincy Adams for a while. The president didn’t know what to do with the alligator, so he put it in a bathtub in the East Room. Visitors and workers at the White House got a little scared when they wandered in and found a big green alligator splashing around in the tub. What would you do if you had an alligator in your bathtub?

“Sometimes presidents were given pets they could not keep in the White House. Martin Van Buren received two tiger cubs from the ruler of a foreign country. President Van Buren really wanted to keep the tiger cubs with him, but Congress decided they would have much more fun at the zoo.

“President James Buchanan was given lots of pets as presents. You see, Buchanan was the only president who never got married. So people thought lots of pets would help keep him company. A king gave him a whole herd of elephants, but Buchanan decided they should live at the zoo. Buchanan also had a pair of bald eagles that he kept at his farm. Buchanan’s favorite pet was a Newfoundland, a very big dog named Lara.

“Abraham Lincoln loved all kinds of animals. When he became president, he got many pets for his children, including ponies, rabbits, and a turkey named Jack. Jack was supposed to be Christmas dinner, but Lincoln’s son Tad fell in love with him and begged his Dad to let him live. Of course, Lincoln could not say no—he loved animals as much as anyone.

"Lincoln also gave Tad two goats named Nanny and Nanko. One day, Tad tied Nanny and Nanko to a kitchen chair and raced through the halls of the White House. Mrs. Lincoln was having a tea party in the East Room when Tad burst in with the goats! President Lincoln tried hard not to laugh, but Mrs. Lincoln did not think it was very funny.

"Many presidents had egg-rolling parties at Easter. Sometimes their pets were included in the fun.

"Andrew Johnson brought two cows with him to the White House when he became president. He also left food out some nights for a family of mice. Ulysses S. Grant had a favorite horse named Butcher Boy, and his daughter, Nellie, had one named Jennie.

"Benjamin Harrison had a frisky goat named Old Whiskers, who would pull his grandchildren around in a cart. One day Old Whiskers took off running with the children in the cart. Harrison and his dog, Dash, had to run very fast to catch them.

"Rutherford B. Hayes and his wife, Lucy, had many pets, including a goat, canaries, dogs, kittens, and a mockingbird. They made the egg roll an official event at the White House every Easter.

“Welcome to the Roosevelt Zoo! Teddy Roosevelt and his six children loved animals, both at the White House and at their family home. One of their pets was a brown and white pony named Algonquin. One time, the president’s son Archie was sick in bed. His brothers, Quentin and Kermit, wanted to cheer him up. Guess what they decided to do? They snuck Algonquin into the White House elevator and up to Archie’s room!

“The Roosevelts also had a bear named Jonathan Edwards, a blue macaw named Eli Yale, a pig named Maude, and a badger named Josiah. They also had cats, dogs, horses, snakes, a kangaroo squirrel, a one-legged rooster, and many other pets—so many pets that the president built a beautiful barn for them on the White House lawn.

“‘Happy Birthday, Laddie Boy!’ Laddie Boy was the favorite dog of President Warren Harding. Harding spoiled him terribly; he even threw Laddie Boy a birthday party with a cake made of dog biscuits covered in white icing.

"When Woodrow Wilson was president, he let his sheep graze on the White House lawn. They kept the lawn mowed by eating the grass until it was nice and short. One of them was named Old Ike, who became famous for chewing tobacco.

"William Howard Taft owned the last cow that lived in the White House. Its name was Pauline Wayne.

"Time for dinner with the Coolidges and their pets! Calvin Coolidge and his wife, Grace, almost had too many pets to count. They often ate in the dining room surrounded by their many animals. When the president yelled 'supper!' the dogs came running.

"They gave their dogs funny names like Calamity Jane, Tiny Tim, and Boston Beans. Grace made elegant floppy hats trimmed with ribbons for their prissy white collie, Prudence Prim, to wear on special occasions.

“The president and Grace also had cats, birds, a donkey, a bobcat, a bear, a wallaby, two lion cubs, and a pygmy hippo. Many of these animals had to live at the zoo because they were a little too wild for the White House.

“Grace hated to keep her birds in a cage, so she let them fly around the White House. One bird even sat on the head of a maid as she did her housework! Coolidge’s favorite pet was a raccoon named Rebecca. Coolidge would put a leash on Rebecca and walk her all around the White House.

"Dogs have always been popular pets with presidents. Some presidents' dogs were not very well behaved. Some were so bad they needed to go to obedience school! One of Franklin D. Roosevelt's dogs, Meg, bit a newspaper reporter on the nose. Another dog named Wink liked to steal bacon from people's breakfast plates.

“Roosevelt’s German shepherd, Major, sometimes bit people. He once ripped the pants of a foreign leader visiting the White House. Roosevelt’s favorite pet was a well-behaved dog named Fala. Fala was a Scottish terrier who became very famous. President Roosevelt took him everywhere, even on trips around the world.

“Time to play at the White House! John F. Kennedy and his wife, Jackie, had many dogs, including a famous one named Pushinka, who came from Russia. Mrs. Kennedy loved animals, especially horses, and so did her daughter, Caroline. Caroline’s favorite pony, named Macaroni, wandered all around the White House lawn.

“Lyndon B. Johnson and his family had many beagles. Two of them were named Him and Her. His favorite dog was Yuki, a mutt from Texas who loved to howl.

"Dwight Eisenhower could have used a howling dog like Yuki. Eisenhower liked to practice golf on the White House lawn. Unfortunately, he had lots of problems with squirrels digging holes in his putting green. Without a dog like Yuki to howl and scare the squirrels away, they kept digging until finally they all had to be captured and taken to a park.

“Welcome home, Mr. President! Nowadays, presidents travel in a helicopter called Marine One. Sometimes their pets are there to meet them when they return to the White House.

“Ronald Reagan had a little spaniel named Rex that would run to meet him and his wife, Nancy, as soon as they landed. President Reagan loved horses; he had five of them. He also had a sheepdog named Lucky that was so big and strong it looked like Mrs. Reagan was water skiing as Lucky dragged her along when she tried to walk him.

"Richard Nixon had Vicky, a poodle; Pasha, a tiny Yorkshire terrier; and King Timahoe, an Irish terrier that liked to shake the hands of people who came to the White House.

"Gerald Ford had a Siamese cat named Chan and a golden retriever named Liberty, who had eight puppies.

"Jimmy Carter also had a Siamese cat.
Its name was Misty Malarkey Ying Yang.
He also had a dog named Grits.

"Let's play catch in the Rose Garden! Presidents George H. W. Bush and his son George W. are both dog lovers. The Bush family loves Springer spaniels, including one named Millie, who had six puppies. One of the puppies, Spotty, was given to George W., who also has a Scottish terrier, Barney, and a black cat named Willie.

"President Bill Clinton and his wife, Hillary, had a dog named Buddy. They also owned a famous cat, Socks, who loved to greet White House visitors.

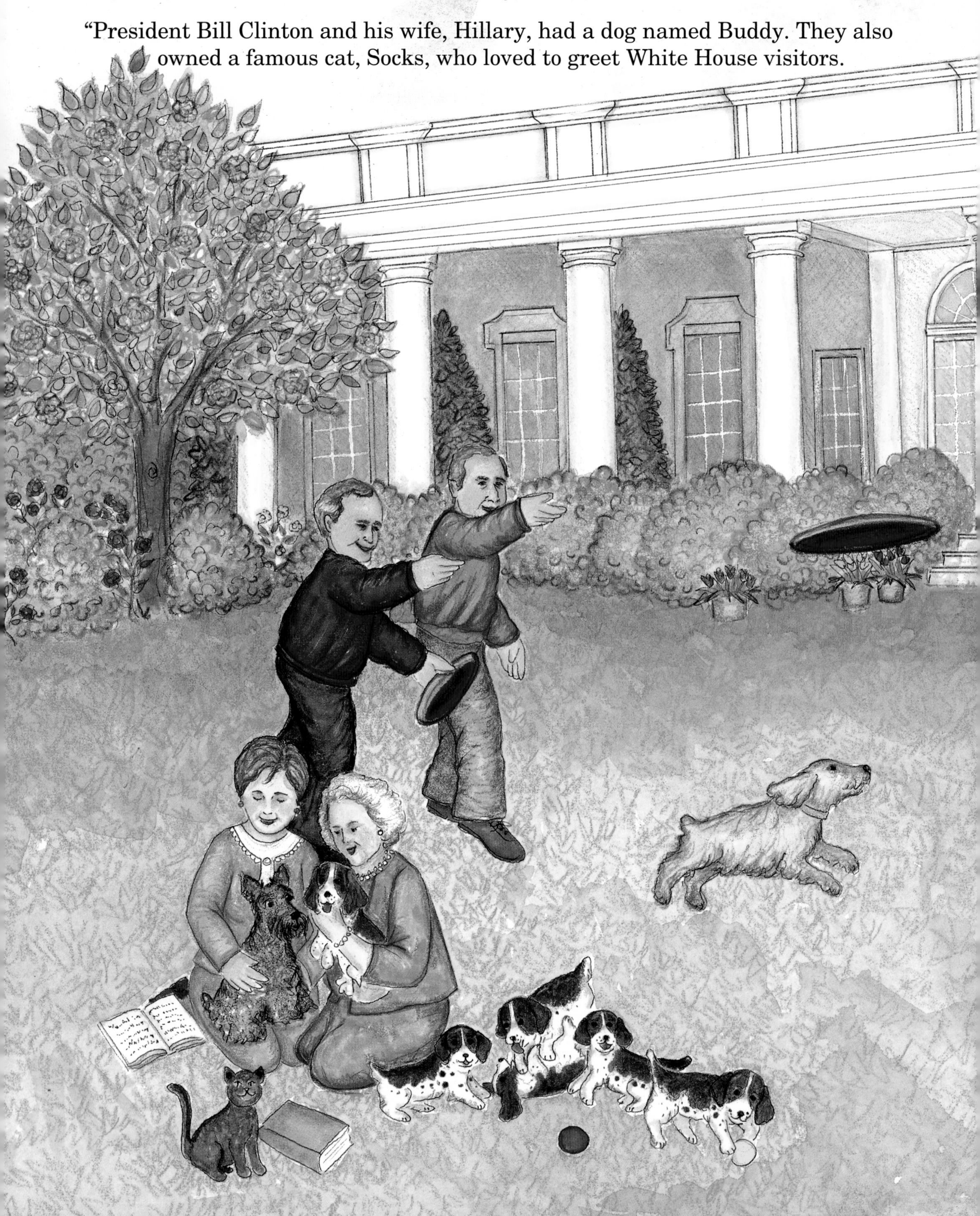

“Malia and Sasha finally got their wish … a Portuguese Water Dog that they named Bo. The President and Mrs. Obama promised them a dog during the 2008 presidential campaign. The First Family planted a vegetable garden at the White House, and Bo wants all children in America to eat more vegetables!

"Wow! Can you believe all the different White House pets the presidents have had over the years?" asked Mrs. Tucker.

"There were dogs, cats, birds, bears, cows, goats, horses, and even an alligator!

"Which White House pet is your favorite? You can use your ballot to vote and tell why you like this pet the most. There are so many fun pets to choose from!"

The Tail End

Resources for Parents and Teachers

No one really knows when humans first started keeping animals as pets, but presidents have sure had a lot of them! Keeping an animal for companionship once was only possible for people like kings who were well off and had the resources to feed extra mouths. Dogs most likely were the first pets because they were easily domesticated. The ancient Romans also kept pets, particularly dogs and birds. Cats and horses were popular with Romans as well and may have been considered pets, but they were also working animals.

The first American settlers brought a few pets with them to the New World, but life was hard in the colonies and resources were scarce. Few people had extra food to give to an animal unless it was earning its keep by working. Some dogs and cats may have been considered pets but were indispensable in performing useful tasks such as hunting, guarding the family farm, or killing unwanted pests. People and businesses needed horses for transportation, as well as public services, who used them for pulling police and fire wagons. Pigs and chickens might seem like cute pets, but people used them mainly as food.

But over time, our ancestors decided to give more animals the status of pets; in many homes and farms, families became less dependent on animals for their work ability.

The modern age of pet keeping began in the mid-1800s, when a thriving middle class emerged in society. This was the first time that many people had the time and money to keep animals solely for companionship.

The Tail End

Resources for Parents and Teachers

President Adams' Alligator introduces many of the favorite pets of the presidents, including dogs, cats, horses, cows, grizzly bears, mockingbirds, parrots, goats, snakes, raccoons, turkeys, sheep, pigs, chickens, roosters—even alligators! Although most pets provide our presidents with a welcome reprieve from their important duties, the alligator kept by President Adams was known for giving White House visitors a good scare!

Presidents such as Martin Van Buren, Theodore Roosevelt, and Calvin Coolidge received gifts of unusual pets from foreign leaders. They included a bobcat, an antelope, a pygmy hippopotamus, two lion cubs, a mynah bird, and a wallaby. While the presidents always acknowledged these gifts with appreciation, the more exotic animals were typically donated to zoos. Nowadays, presidential families generally choose cats and dogs as their pets.

Fortunately, the White House sits on 18 acres of lush grounds—plenty of room for most pets to play.

From George Washington's cherished horse Nelson to President Obama's dog Bo, these unelected White House residents have often been among the most popular members of presidential families! But to busy presidents in particular, they may hold a special place in their hearts. "If animals gave them a moment's relaxation or a short respite from continual burdens," wrote Margaret Truman, the daughter of President Harry Truman, "Then I think they're worth remembering for that reason if for no other."

Presidential Pets Matching Game

Match the pet to its description.

A. **Pushinka**—Mixed-breed puppy from Russia, given to Caroline Kennedy by Soviet Premier Nikita Khrushchev. Pushinka means "fluffy" in Russian.

____

B. **Nanny**—One of the goats that pulled the Lincoln children around the White House grounds in a cart. Goats were kept by many presidents during earlier years.

____

C. **Nelson**—Chestnut horse. George Washington's horse during the Revolutionary War. George and Martha Washington did not live in the White House.

____

D. **Pauline**—The last cow to live at the White House. Milk cow for William H. Taft. Pauline supplied milk for the personal use of President Taft and his family.

____

E. **Bo**—Portuguese Water Dog given to Malia and Sasha Obama by the late Senator Ted Kennedy.

____

F. **Laddie Boy**—Airedale owned by Warren G. Harding. Laddie Boy had his own big chair to sit in during cabinet meetings. Laddie Boy was Harding's constant companion.

G. **Rob Roy**—White collie owned by Grace Coolidge. The Coolidges had one of the largest collections of pets ever to live in the White House.

____

H. **Spot**, English springer spaniel, and **Barney**—White House dogs of George W. and Laura Bush.

____

I. **Sheep**—Woodrow Wilson kept a small flock of sheep on the White House grounds in order to keep the grass mowed during WWI.

____

J. **Him** and **Her**—Twin beagles owned by Lyndon B. Johnson. They loved to play in the Oval Office and race down the halls.

____

K. **Rebecca**—Raccoon who stayed in the outdoor shed at night and occasionally roamed the White House during the day. Owned by Calvin and Grace Coolidge.

____

L. **Liberty**—Golden retriever owned by Gerald Ford. Mother of eight pups that were born in the White House.

____

Answer Key **A.** 7, **B.** 11, **C.** 8, **D.** 1, **E.** 10, **F.** 3, **G.** 5, **H.** 12, **I.** 2, **J.** 4, **K.** 6, **L.** 9

Presidential Pets Fact or Fiction

Which of the following statements are true?

True False Millie, the pet English springer spaniel of President George H. W. Bush, was the first presidential dog to write a book (co-authored by First Lady Barbara Bush).

True False President Coolidge was known to walk a raccoon named Rebecca around the White House on a leash.

True False A statue of Fala, President Franklin D. Roosevelt's favorite dog, stands beside a statue of his presidential owner at the Franklin Delano Roosevelt Memorial.

True False Ernie, an orange and white cat rescued by President George W. Bush when he was governor of Texas, had six toes.

True False Liberty, President Gerald Ford's golden retriever, gave birth to eight puppies while living in the White House.

True False President James Buchanan's 170-pound Newfoundland, Lara, is the biggest dog so far to live in the White House.

True False President Lyndon Johnson danced with Yuki, a stray mutt found at a gas station, at his daughter Luci's wedding.

True False President Abraham Lincoln's dog Fido was the first presidential dog to be photographed.

True False President Ronald Reagan had a King Charles spaniel named Rex who lived in a designer doghouse with photos of his famous parents on the walls.

True False President Theodore Roosevelt had the most White House pets, which reportedly included five dogs, two cats, twelve horses, five guinea pigs, five bears, several pet snakes, assorted lizards, two kangaroo rats, several roosters, an owl, a macaw, a flying squirrel, a raccoon, a pony, a coyote, a lion, a hyena, a zebra, a badger, and a rat.

True False Major, President Franklin D. Roosevelt's German shepherd, once tried to rip off the British prime minister's pants.

True False President Warren Harding's family celebrated their dog Laddie Boy's birthday by inviting other dogs to a party and serving a dog biscuit cake.

Answer Key If you answered true to all twelve statements, you are absolutely 100% correct! You are also correct if you noticed that our presidents have quite a history of pampering their pets!

Bibliography

Bausum, Ann. *Our Country's Presidents.* Washington: National Geographic Society, 2001.

Blue, Rose, and Corine J. Naden. *The White House Kids.* Brookfield: The Millbrook Press, 1995.

Bowman, John. *The History of the American Presidency.* Rev. ed. North Dighton: World Publications Group, 2002.

Kelly, Niall. *Presidential Pets.* New York: Abbeville Press, 1992.

Kunhardt, Philip B., Jr., Philip B. Kunhardt III and Peter W. Kunhardt. *The American President.* New York: Riverhead Books, 1999.

Leiner, Katherine. *First Children: Growing Up in the White House.* New York: Tambourine Books, 1996.

Rowan, Roy, and Brooke Janis. *First Dogs: American Presidents and Their Best Friends.* Chapel Hill: Algonquin Books of Chapel Hill, 1997.

Seale, William. *The President's House.* 2 vols. Washington: White House Historical Association, 1986.

Truman, Margaret. *White House Pets.* New York: David McKay Company, Inc., 1969.

Resources for Pet People

Our presidents loved their pets! So do lots of other Americans. According to the American Pet Products Association, 62 percent of American households have at least one pet. In other words, we have 78.2 million dogs and about 86.4 million cats running around our homes! And that doesn't include all the hamsters, birds, ferrets, and other animals that us humans take home as pets.

Not every pet is lucky enough to find a home where it is cared for and loved. Every year approximately five to seven million dogs and cats enter animal shelters around the nation. Some of these animals get separated from their owners without tags, tattoos, or microchips to identify them. Some are strays who are picked up by animal control. Others simply aren't wanted by their families anymore.

If you have a pet, here are some ways to take good care of it:

- Get them spayed or neutered.
- Brush their hair and keep them clean.
- Feed and water them every day.
- Walk and play with them every day.
- Train your pet to behave properly.

You can find all kinds of good pet care advice at the PBS Kids website.

If you don't have a pet and your family decides it's time to get one, consider adopting a pet from your local animal shelter or animal rescue organizations. Research different types of breeds to make sure you choose a pet that is likely to fit in with your family's lifestyle. For instance, if you live in a small apartment you probably won't want to choose a 120-pound Newfoundland—even if it is absolutely adorable!

To find a local animal shelter, go online to the American Society for the Prevention of Cruelty to Animals (ASPCA).

To find out more about presidential pets, visit websites for:

- the Presidential Pet Museum
- the White House
- the Animal Planet / Discovery Channel

The Idea Behind President Adams' Alligator

In February 2002, I was called by First Lady Laura Bush's office and asked if I would illustrate the 2002 White House Holiday Program. It took me about half a second to say...yes! What an honor! It took months of research and many trips to the White House meeting with members of the Bush staff to create the illustrations for "All Creatures Great and Small." The program tells the story of the many pets that have lived at the White House.

Once the holidays were over, I decided to use all the information I had collected and create a presidential pets book that would excite, delight, and teach kids about our U.S. presidents and their pets!

Cheryl Shaw Barnes

Acknowledgments

We wish to thank former First Lady Laura Bush and members of her staff for their support and encouragement in creating the program which inspired this book. Also, many thanks to the supportive team at Regnery Kids including Marji Ross, Diane Lindsey Reeves, Emily Kephart, Lisa Pulaski, Maria Ruhl, Amanda Larsen, Amber Colleran, Tess Civantos, and Ryan Pando.

Dear Fellow Pet Lovers,

Wayne Hulehan

President Adams' Alligator has been one of our favorite books to write and illustrate because we love pets! When Cheryl was a little girl, she would find and bring home stray animals—everything from turtles and squirrels to birds, kittens, and many a dog... and even a duck named Peeps.

Over the years we've adopted dozens of pets, all sharing one thing in common: they were all rescue animals. Sometimes we would find them at our local animal shelter and sometimes they would find us.

Recently Cheryl discovered a mommy cat and her three kittens living beneath our porch. We knew it was important to get them spayed and neutered to help them live a longer and happier life and also to help reduce pet overpopulation. But, first we had to make friends with them. We started setting out bowls of food. Before we knew it they had become beloved members of our family and quite entertaining too!

We would especially like to thank the animal welfare workers at the Vola Lawson Animal Shelter in our home town for giving us help and guidance with our rescue cats.

If you ever decide you want a pet, please go to your local animal shelter first. You are sure to find just the right pet that will give you many years of entertainment, companionship, and unconditional love.

We hope you've enjoyed our book!

Peter and Cheryl Barnes
with Woody B and Zoe

Vote for Your Favorite White House Pet

Use this ballot to vote for your favorite one and explain why you like this pet the most.

Write a Short Story about a Favorite Pet

Pretend a pet you know is invited to visit the White House. Make up a short story about its adventures. Have fun!